First published in Belgium and Holland by Clavis Uitgeverij, Hasselt – Amsterdam, 2014
Copyright © 2014, Clavis Uitgeverij

English translation from the Dutch by Clavis Publishing Inc. New York
Copyright © 2015 for the English language edition: Clavis Publishing Inc. New York

Visit us on the web at www.clavisbooks.com

Pinocchio's Dream written and illustrated by An Leysen
Original title: *De droom van Pinocchio*
Translated from the Dutch by Clavis Publishing

ISBN 978-1-60537-224-2

This book was printed in April 2015 at Proost Industries NV,
Everdongenlaan 23, 2300 Turnhout, Belgium

First Edition
10 9 8 7 6 5 4 3 2 1

PINOCCHIO'S DREAM

An Leysen

Clavis

NEW YORK

ONCE UPON A TIME there was a carpenter named Gepetto. He lived all by himself in a small room with one tiny window to let in the light. There was only one wobbly chair in the room and a broken table, which Gepetto used as a bed at night. There also was an open hearth with a fire. But the flames were painted, just like the bowl of soup that seemed to be simmering above them.

GEPETTO often felt lonely is his little room. One day he decided to make a puppet. A wooden puppet that could dance and sing like a real acrobat and that could keep him company. Gepetto had a piece of wood lying about that would be just right. He got all his tools together and started cutting and carving and sanding. The carpenter first made the little body. Then he made two legs, two arms, two hands, two feet and finally the head.

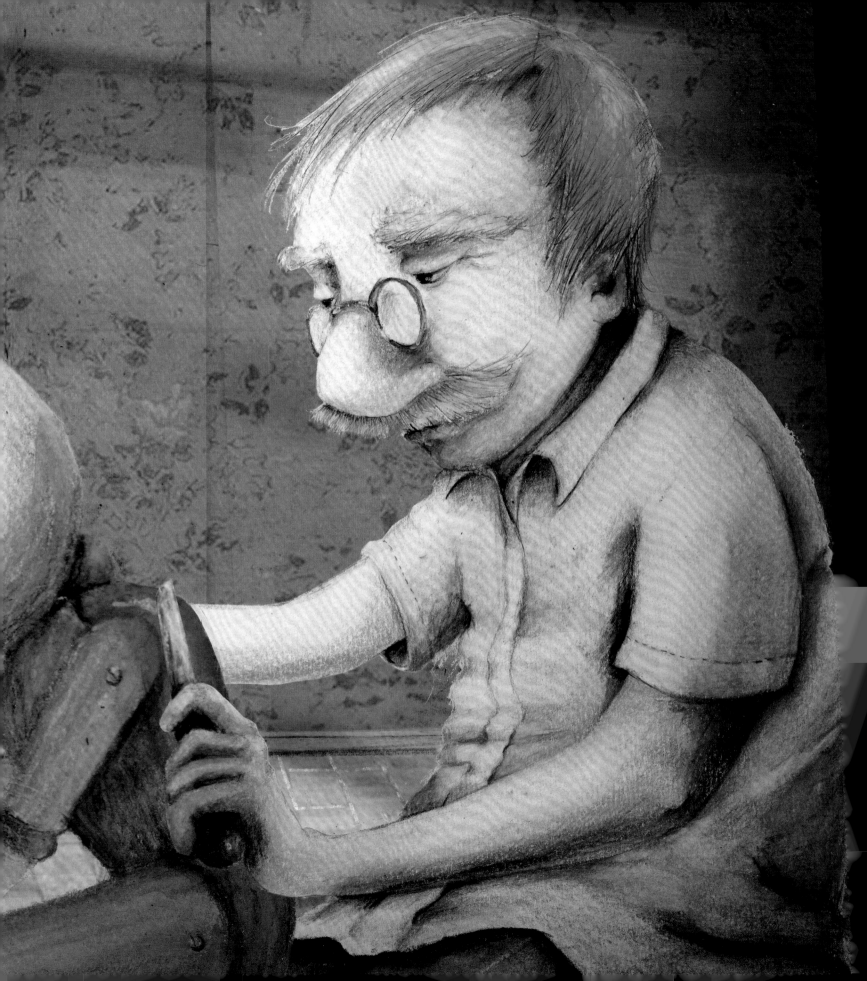

GEPETTO worked on his puppet's eyes for a really long time. When he finished them, it seemed as if they were really looking at him. After that he made the nose, but just when Gepetto thought it looked perfect, the nose started to grow. It grew and grew until it almost grew out through the little window. Gepetto shook his head in amazement and cut off a big piece of the wooden nose, but it immediately grew back again. And that happened each and every time Gepetto tried to shorten the nose. Eventually the old man called out in anger:

"Confounded nose, if you do not stop that right now, I will turn you into firewood."

It was as if the puppet could understand him, because the nose immediately shrunk to a normal size and Gepetto was able to continue working.

The PUPPET'S MOUTH wasn't even finished, when it started laughing loudly: "Ha ha, ho ho…. Stop that, it tickles!" Gepetto was so scared that he almost fell off his chair. Did that mouth just speak to him? It must have been his imagination! Maybe it was solitude which was making him hear things that weren't really there.

But when Gepetto tried to finish the wooden ears with his knife, the same voice called really loudly:

"Ouch! You're hurting me!"

And the puppet gave him a hard kick.

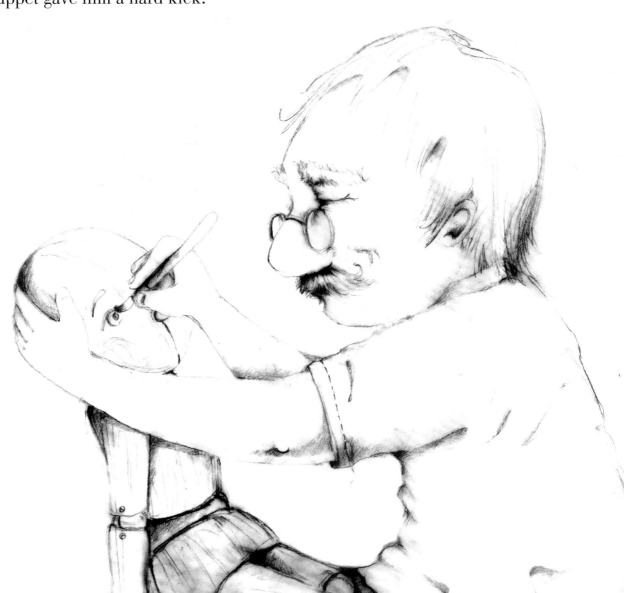

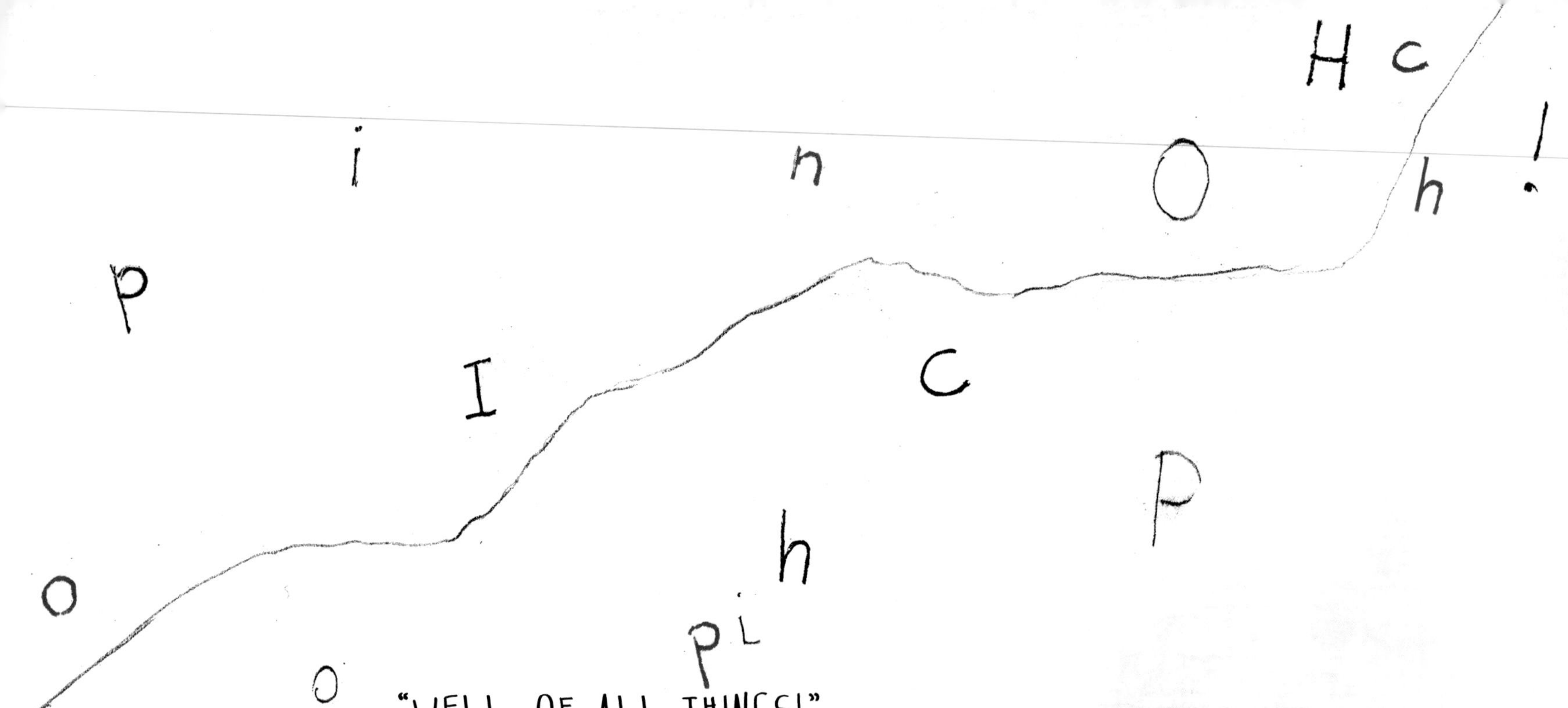

p i n O H c h !

P I C P

o o p L h

"**WELL, OF ALL THINGS!**" Gepetto shouted. **"That puppet is alive!**
I'd better give him a name." The carpenter thought long and hard.
"How about Charles?"

"Oh, no," the puppet answered. "That's so dull."

"I could name you John or Jeff or Pete."

"Definitely not! There are already so many boys with that name.

N i **I want a special name."**

GEPETTO thought of more than a hundred names,
but the puppet kept shaking his head. "No! No! No!
You'll have to do better than that!"

"CONFOUNDED RASCAL!" Gepetto grumbled eventually.
"Whether you agree with it or not, I am going to call you **Pi-noc-chi-o**
and that's it!"

Now that Pinocchio had a name
all he needed were some clothes.
Gepetto, who was really poor and didn't
have a cent in his pocket, sewed a pair of
pants and a little sweater from two
old pieces of cloth. He stripped
off some wallpaper to make
a waistcoat and finally folded
a little hat out of newspaper.

GEPETTO'S HOUSE

PINOCCHIO was a beautiful puppet, but he didn't want to dangle from strings. He wanted to be a real boy. He wanted to run and jump, he wanted to go outside, to see the world. But if he was to be a real boy, he had a lot to learn. "Dear Daddy Gepetto," he begged in his sweetest voice. "I no longer want to be a puppet; I want to go to school. But to do that, I will need books…." Gepetto sighed, he didn't have the money to buy books. But when he saw tears well up in Pinocchio's eyes, he quickly put on his old velvet jacket that was fraying at the sleeves and collar, and which had holes everywhere, and he walked outside.

SCHOOL →

GEPETTO returned home after a half hour, carrying a big schoolbook. He was shivering because it was snowing outside and he was wearing just his sweater.

"Where is your jacket, Daddy Gepetto?" Pinocchio asked, worried.

"I sold it," Gepetto answered. "Soon it will be spring anyway."

Pinocchio hugged the carpenter and gave him a kiss on the cheek.

The next day Pinocchio left for school early. In one hand he held a nice, shiny apple and in the other he held his new schoolbook.

PINOCCHIO hadn't even arrived at the school gate
when he stumbled upon two strange characters:
a cat that was blind in one eye, and a crippled fox.
At first sight they looked really grand and
distinguished in their fancy suits, but if you looked
closer you could see the rips in their
jackets and the nasty look in their eyes.

Those two were up to no good!

"HELLO, SWEET BOY," the cat flattered.

"That's a nice book you've got there."

The fox looked at the apple hungrily.

"Good morning, Mister Cat and Gentleman Fox,"
Pinocchio answered politely. "I am heading for school,
and there I am going to learn everything that's in this
book. I will learn how to read and write and do math.
And when all that studying has made me hungry,
I will eat this tasty apple."

"O, LITTLE BOY!" the cat started moaning. "Don't go to school, nothing good ever comes from it! Just look at me and my friend Fox. We were always good boys and worked hard in school and what became of us? All that reading blinded me in one eye, and my friend here got a lame leg when a heavy book fell on it. Trust me, reading and doing math gets you nowhere in life. It's much better to do whatever you feel like doing and to have fun. There happens to be a puppet show in town today. Why don't you go and take a look?"

A PUPPET SHOW! Pinocchio thought about his sweet Daddy Gepetto, who had sold his only jacket to buy him a schoolbook. He didn't want to disappoint him. But he had his whole life to go to school and he had never seen a puppet show before. Maybe he could go and have a quick look, just for a moment….

"Why don't you just give your book to me," the cat said slyly. **"I will hold on to it for you."**

With a quick movement the fox snatched the apple from Pinocchio's hand. And while Pinocchio headed to the show, the two villains quickly took to their heels.

AS HE DREW NEAR TO THE SHOW, Pinocchio heard laughter and singing. It seemed like a lively place.

HARLEQUIN was pretending to be in love with a beautiful princess, and he was singing her a song when he caught sight of Pinocchio.

HARLEQUIN immediately stopped singing and bowed to Pinocchio laughing:

"Welcome, welcome, sweet puppet boy,
how nice of you to pay us a visit!"

The other puppets wanted to greet Pinocchio as well and they all called out at the same time, which ruined the show and made the crowd jeer and leave.

THE PUPPETEER, who watched it all helplessy, was furious.

"You little squirt!" he roared.
"How dare you make such a mess of my show?
I will teach you a lesson!"

THE PUPPETEER grabbed hold of Pinocchio. "Oh my," he muttered in amazement. **"You are a very special puppet!** You move and walk without anyone pulling the strings! You will work for me and you will make me a very rich man!"

PINOCCHIO had to take part in the puppet show each and every day. From far and wide people came to see the puppet that could sing and dance without anyone pulling the strings. The wooden puppet did wonderful tricks and soon became the public's favorite. Pinocchio was famous, and he enjoyed it.

But as soon as the show was over, the puppeteer locked him up in a small cage to make sure he couldn't escape. Then Pinocchio felt lonely, and he thought about Gepetto.

He missed his Daddy.

"Oh, if only I had been a good boy and gone to school," Pinocchio sighed. "I'd be home with Daddy Gepetto instead of sitting in this cage." Big tears rolled down his wooden cheeks.

Because of the tears he didn't see the pretty girl with long hair who was standing in front of his cage.

It was the Blue Fairy, who had heard his crying and felt sorry for the poor puppet.

WITH ONE SWEEP of her magic wand she opened the cage door.
"Hello sweet boy, tell me why you are being held here."

AT FIRST, Pinocchio was so impressed by the beauty of the Blue Fairy that he could not utter a single word. But pretty soon he started talking nineteen to the dozen about how he was once a regular piece of wood and how Gepetto used that piece of wood to make a puppet. And how Gepetto had put in so much love that the puppet had come to life and could walk and talk all by himself. Pinocchio also explained how the mean puppeteer had captured him and how he had to perform during the day and was locked in a cage at night, so that he couldn't escape.

"It's not fair!" Pinocchio concluded his story.
"I have been nothing but good and honest!"

THAT WAS A LIE OF COURSE,

because Pinocchio had promised Gepetto that he would go to school and he went to see the puppet show instead. And he'd given his schoolbook, for which Gepetto had sold his jacket, to the cat. Before he finished his story, Pinocchio felt his nose itching. He had the strange feeling that his nose was growing.

Oh, it wasn't just a feeling, his nose really was growing! Longer and longer!

"My, my," the fairy spoke sternly. "You are a little fibber! Your nose tells me you're not being completely honest."

PINOCCHIO STARTED TO CRY.

And because the Blue Fairy was a good fairy,
and because she was tired of his crying,
she worked magic to bring Pinocchio's nose back to a normal size.

"From now on, you're not allowed to lie," the Blue Fairy told him sternly.
"You have to do what your father tells you, or you will get in trouble.
But if you're a good puppet, then you will be rewarded for sure!
Now, go back home. And hurry, because Daddy Gepetto
is probably worried sick about you!"

Pinocchio thanked the Blue Fairy and ran as quickly
as his little puppet legs could carry him. But the road home
was long, and Pinocchio got tired from all the walking.
He decided to take a rest on the side of the road.

PINOCCHIO was enjoying the wintry sun, which slowly warmed his cold little puppet body. After about an hour or so, he saw two familiar characters approaching: the cat and the fox.

"**A very good day, young man,**" the cat greeted him in a friendly way. "What a pleasant coincidence that we should run into you again. But tell me, what brings you to this place?"

"Hello Mister Cat and Gentleman Fox," Pinocchio answered politely. "I was on my way home. You see, I worked for the puppet show for a little while and became famous, but I missed my sweet Daddy Gepetto."

"Ah, work," the cat said superciliously. "That's for dumb people. I would never do that, it makes your hands coarse and your back sore. No, we prefer to take it easy and yet we are never hungry. Isn't that right, comrade Fox?"

THE FOX DIDN'T SAY A WORD. He just growled and nodded his agreement. "But how do you get the money to buy food and drink and clothes?"

"Well, sweet boy, that's our little secret… but if you happen to have a coin on you, we would be happy to share it with you."

Pinocchio actually did have a golden coin on him, one that the puppeteer had slipped him in a generous mood. The cat and the fox couldn't believe their eyes when they saw how the sunlight reflected off the beautiful coin in Pinocchio's hand.

"PLEASE, MISTER CAT! PLEASE, GENTLEMAN FOX,"

Pinocchio begged. "Tell me your secret. That way I will never have to work again and yet still be able to buy everything I need. And with the money that's left, I will buy a new winter coat for my Daddy."

"We'd be happy to, but first you have to follow us to the land of mopers and nincompoops."

"I have never heard of that! Where is it?"

"Somewhere in between far away and nearby. But don't rack your little brain over that.
Just follow us and do what we tell you to do."

THEY WALKED FOR A FULL HOUR, and then fifteen minutes more. The cat in front, Pinocchio in the middle, and the fox in the rear, as if he wanted to make sure that Pinocchio didn't sneak off.

It was starting to get dark when they reached a big meadow with a huge tree right in the middle.

"This is it!" the cat called excitedly, and he did a little dance. Pinocchio wanted to dance along, but his feet hurt too much from walking. The cat ran out to the meadow and dug a little hole in between the roots of the tree. He put Pinocchio's coin into it, filled it up, then poured some water over it.

PINOCCHIO WATCHED. "Now what?"

"Now we have to wait for the big tree to grow coins just like the golden one we have buried. If you're lucky, it might be a thousand coins. If not, at least a hundred! Why don't you take a nap, and I promise that you will be rich when you wake up!"

SILLY PINOCCHIO believed the words of the cat and the fox, and he forgot his promise to the Blue Fairy.

Using moss and fallen leaves, Pinocchio built a cozy little nest for himself against a tree at the edge of the meadow. He lay down and was asleep within minutes.

It was still early when the first sunbeams woke him. He jumped up and hurried to the big tree. But he was disappointed: there wasn't a single golden coin hanging on the branches.

WELL, OF COURSE, PINOCCHIO THOUGHT, Mister Cat and Gentleman Fox didn't realize that it was winter and in winter nothing grows on trees! Pinocchio could have kicked himself. He decided to dig up the coin and to try again in spring.

But no matter how hard Pinocchio searched, he couldn't find his golden coin. Of course, those two bandits had run off with it!

PINOCCHIO wanted to go back home, and this time he was determined to stick to the straight and narrow path. He would not to be tempted by anything!

He walked until he came to a small village. At the market square, there were lots of people milling around. Everybody was busy working.

I don't like this village at all, Pinocchio thought. *I am just a wooden puppet, I wasn't made to work that hard.* He would have preferred to leave immediately, but because his stomach was rumbling with hunger, he decided to find something to eat first.

A MAN PASSED BY, pulling two heavy carts all by himself.

The man was panting and puffing, and he had to stop every few steps to wipe the sweat off his forehead with a handkerchief. Pinocchio walked towards him. "Hello sir, could you spare me some change so I could buy something to eat? **I am very hungry.**"

"I'd be happy to give you some money, little boy," the man answered, "if you help me pull these heavy carts." Pinocchio looked at the man indignantly. He was no workhorse! He looked round the marketplace again, and saw a woman carrying a basket full of dirty clothes. "Hey lady," he called, "would you happen to have something for me to nibble on?"

"SURE, SWEET BOY," the woman said,
"but first you'll have to help me bring this basket of clothes to the laundry.'
"But that basket looks so heavy," Pinocchio grumbled. "I don't want to get tired."
"You little lazybones," the woman said.
"If you won't work, you won't eat either!"

PINOCCHIO asked at least twenty other people if they would give him some food or some money, but they all said he had to work for it first.
Finally he met a little lady, carrying two big jugs of milk.
"Can I please have a sip of milk?" Pinocchio begged, because by now he wasn't just hungry, but he was terribly thirsty too.
The little lady felt sorry for the wooden puppet and let him drink as much as he wanted.
"Aaah," Pinocchio smacked his lips, "that was delicious.
If only I could have something to eat as well…."
"If you carry one of these jugs to my home, then I will make us a terrific meal: tomato soup and cauliflower and a tender piece of chicken." Pinocchio's mouth watered.
Gee, that sounded delicious!
But those jugs of milk did look very heavy…. "And for dessert," the little lady continued, "there will be ice cream with chocolate sauce and plenty of whipped cream."
Now Pinocchio was convinced. Suddenly he looked as strong as two men put together.
Carrying the heavy jug of milk, he ran to the little lady's house.

PINOCCHIO gulped down all the food greedily. Only when he took the last mouthful of ice cream, did he look up to thank the sweet little lady. "Ooo!" he said, staring at her with his spoon still in his hand and his mouth filled with chocolate sauce.

"But… but you… you… you are…" he stammered.

"You are the Blue Fairy!"

THE FAIRY LOOKED AT HIM STERNLY.

"Pinocchio, Pinocchio," she said.

"Will you ever become an honest boy?"

"Oh, but I want to become a good boy," Pinocchio answered.

"I want that a lot, actually, because I'm tired of being a wooden puppet."

"You can't become a real boy until you prove that you deserve it."

"How?"

"By trying really hard, and by being good and obedient."

"OH, I ALREADY AM ALL THOSE THINGS,"
Pinocchio said.
But before he finished talking,
his nose started to grow again.
Pinocchio blushed and
he stammered shyly:

"Well, sometimes…
anyways… I try to."

"I know that," the fairy smiled.
"But you'll have to try even harder."
And she worked her magic to bring
Pinocchio's nose back to its regular length.

PINOCCHIO had a normal nose again, and he promised the fairy that he would be a good boy who wouldn't play any more silly tricks. He also promised that he would go straight home and back to school. He took off in good spirits.

AFTER HE HAD WALKED FOR HALF A DAY,

Pinocchio was almost run over by a cart jam-packed with little boys. The coachman drove the cart over the small pathway, and the boys cheered and sang:

"We're going to the Land of Must-Nothing and Can-Everything!

Quickly jump on board and come along with us!" Pinocchio hesitated. The Land of Must-Nothing and Can-Everything, sounded almost too good to be true! But he thought about what he had promised the fairy.

THE COACHMAN HAD STOPPED.

"Hey little boy," he called, "how about it? I don't have all day!"

The boys in the back all started talking at the same time: "We're heading towards the nicest land in the whole world, it's always a holiday there. You never have to eat nasty things and you can have all the candy you want! There are no teachers or parents telling you what you can or can't do. You never have to get up early. There are more toys than you ever dared to dream about."
Wow! That's a place I have to see with my own eyes, Pinocchio thought and he jumped on the cart.

"Whoopee! Off we go!"

THE BOYS HADN'T EXAGGERATED.

The Land of Must-Nothing and Can-Everything really was a children's paradise.
Pinocchio had the time of his life there. He filled his belly with candy and other
treats and he played with the other children from dusk until dawn. Time flew –
the way it tends to when you're having fun.

BUT ONE MORNING, when Pinocchio got up, he felt a bit funny. His whole body

itched and tickled. He felt as if he were being pulled from all sides. And then his
little paper hat started to rise. He jumped and touched his head and his ears. Oh
goodness! What was happening? His ears were growing! They were pointy and
covered in fluffy hair. Pinocchio was filled with shame. He pulled his little hat
downwards so no one could see those ugly ears. But then he noticed that his pants
were ripping at the back.

He had a tail!
"Help!" the wooden boy cried. "He-eelp! Hie-eelp! Hi-eaa! Heehaw!"

His calling turned into the loud braying of a donkey. Oh my, that was his punishment
for not listening to the fairy! Instead of going to school and studying hard
like he promised, he had been playing and loafing about.

And now he was turning into a dumb donkey
instead of into a smart boy!

WITH TEARS IN HIS EYES, Pinocchio ran as fast as he could.
He ran and ran until he reached the sea and the Land of Must-Nothing
and Can-Everything was far behind him. Even then he kept running,
and he finally dove into the ice-cold water with a big splash.
To his relief, he felt his tail shrinking and his long ears
returning to normal.

Pinocchio was once again a wooden puppet.
Thank goodness, because wood floats and Pinocchio
had never learned how to swim.

PINOCCHIO spent a few days bobbing up and down in the sea. Sometimes a seagull would drop a tasty little fish and the boy would eat it eagerly. Just when he started to get a bit seasick from all that floating, a giant monster appeared on the horizon.

IT WAS AN ENORMOUS WHALE, the biggest one you could possibly imagine. The animal had a huge mouth, which he stretched wide open. Pinocchio splashed about, but he couldn't escape.

The whale swallowed him down in one big gulp.

IT WAS SO DARK IN THE BELLY OF THE WHALE it seemed as if Pinocchio had fallen into a pot of black paint. But somewhere in the distance he saw a little light. Pinocchio shuffled over cautiously. The closer he got to the light, the more he could see. A shadow… A man sitting on something… An old man sitting on a box and eating. It was… Gepetto. His dear Daddy Gepetto!

Pinocchio fell upon the carpenter and hugged him so hard that Gepetto could barely breathe. Of course, Gepetto was overjoyed to see Pinocchio again too. He had been looking for his boy all the time that Pinocchio had been away! Gepetto had looked in every village and every city, and finally he had built a little boat to go and look for Pinocchio out at sea. Unfortunately, the whale had swallowed him. Fortunately, it was a gluttonous whale who gulped down whole schools of fish at once, so Gepetto always had enough to eat. But now that he found Pinocchio, Gepetto wanted to go home with his son. Back to his small, comfy little room.

"Sweet Daddy," Pinocchio said, "we'll have to escape."

"Escape? But how, Pinocchio? There is no way out, and even if there was, I can't swim!"

"DON'T WORRY ABOUT THAT, DADDY." As quick as lightning, Pinocchio folded his paper hat into a boat that was just big enough for them both. "When the whale opens his huge mouth to swallow his next meal, we'll jump out. We'll jump straight into the sea and paddle to the shore in this little boat."

No sooner said than done. They climbed all the way from the belly to the back of the whale's throat. When the whale opened his mouth, they dove into the sea. The whale was so busy eating that he didn't even notice what was happening. By the time the animal got hungry again, Pinocchio and Gepetto were long gone.

THE SEA WAS CHOPPY and the coast was still far away. Gepetto lay in the little boat, shivering with exhaustion and cold, while Pinocchio paddled towards the mainland on his own. After a while, Pinocchio noticed that water was seeping into the little paper boat.

THE BOAT KEPT GETTING HEAVIER and Pinocchio knew that it wouldn't be able to float for much longer. Just when it seemed as if all was lost, an enormous wave lifted them up and carried them to the beach. **They were safe!** Relieved but exhausted, Pinocchio closed his eyes.

"PINOCCHIO, PINOCCHIO, RISE AND SHINE!"
Sunbeams shone on his face.
It was as if they were trying to wake him by tickling him.

Pinocchio opened his eyes.
He wasn't at the beach anymore.
He was lying in a lovely soft bed underneath a warm blanket,
and the sun was shining through the curtains into a small,
messy, boy's room. Pinocchio felt a bit strange.
Different. He looked at his hands, touched his face.

He wasn't a wooden puppet anymore.
  He was a real boy!

DELIRIOUSLY HAPPY, he jumped from his bed and ran out of his room, down the stairs, and into the kitchen. **"Finally, you're up, sleepyhead! It's nearly time to go to school. Eat your breakfast quickly!"**

His mother smiled merrily. Her face looked exactly like the face of **the Blue Fairy**.
On the other side of the table, a man looked up to him from behind his newspaper.
It was… Daddy Gepetto!